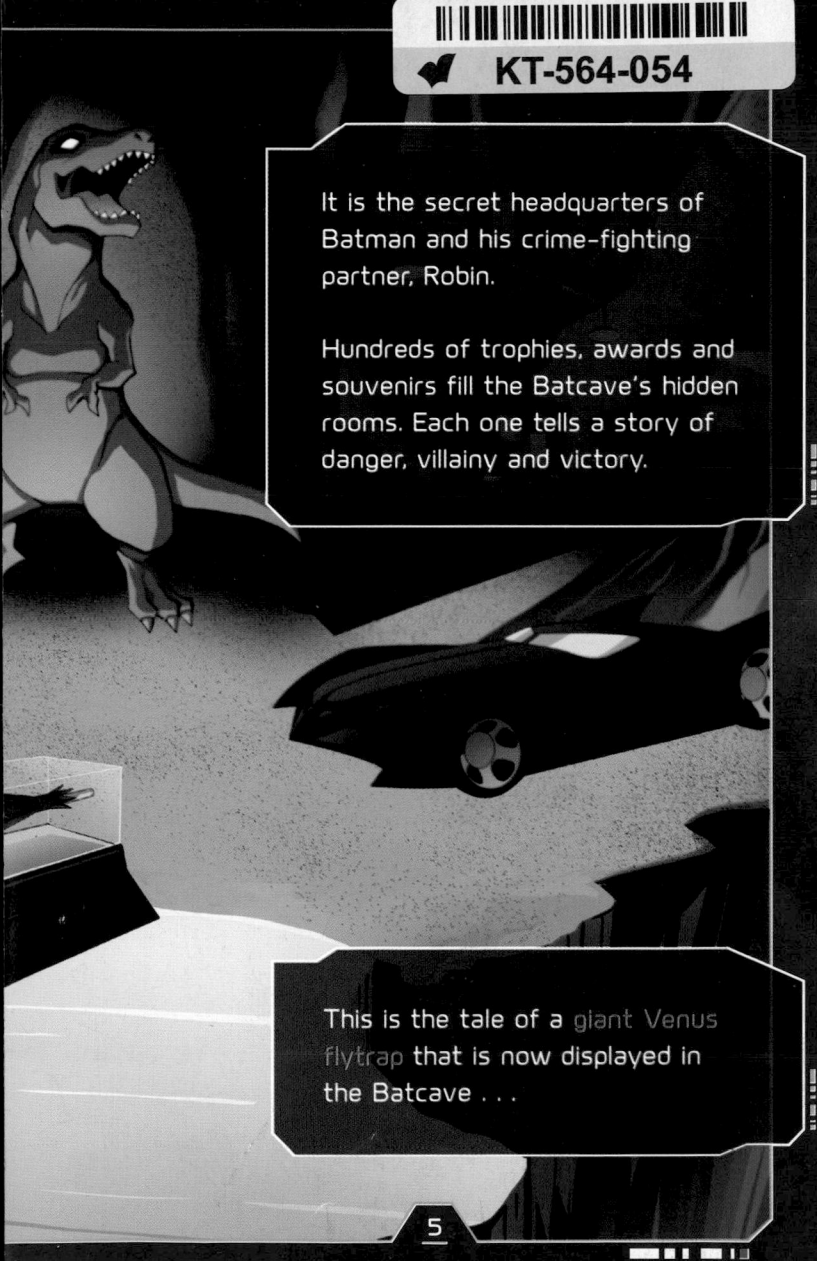

It is the secret headquarters of Batman and his crime-fighting partner, Robin.

Hundreds of trophies, awards and souvenirs fill the Batcave's hidden rooms. Each one tells a story of danger, villainy and victory.

This is the tale of a giant Venus flytrap that is now displayed in the Batcave . . .

CONTENTS

This is the BATCAVE.

GIANT VENUS FLYTRAP

4

CHAPTER 1

NIGHT SOUNDS

Tree branches sway and shiver outside the prison walls of Arkham Asylum.

The branches move, but there is no wind to move them.

From a window high in one wall, a strange song drifts through the night air.

Garcia, a prison guard, gazes up at the sealed glass window.

Why is Poison Ivy singing? the guard wonders. *It sounds like a lullaby.*

Then the lullaby suddenly stops.

Garcia hears another sound. Something rustles in the trees a few metres away.

Garcia whispers into his radio. "I need backup," he says. "Quick. Something funny's going on out here!"

Moments later, the prison alarm goes off.

RIII-IIIIIII-IIIIIII-IIINGGG!

The window in Poison Ivy's cell is gone.
It has been replaced by a large, jagged hole.

Stones and rubble lie on the ground below
the window.

The trees have stopped swaying. Poison Ivy is
nowhere to be found.

PLANT OR ANIMAL?

The alarm bells are still ringing when the Batmobile roars up to the prison.

The Dynamic Duo swiftly follows the guards to the back of the building.

The Boy Wonder stares at the jagged hole in the wall. "How did she do it, Batman?" he asks.

"Batman! Robin!" cries the prison doctor. "I'm so glad you're here!" The doctor is kneeling by the moaning Garcia.

"I found this in Garcia's arm," the doctor says. She holds up a sharp object. "He woke up as soon as I pulled it out of his skin."

Batman holds the object in his glove.
"It looks like a fang," he says.

The hero pulls a small device from his Utility
Belt. He scans the mysterious object.

"Is it from a wild animal?" asks Robin.

Batman reads the display on his device. "The computer at the Batcave thinks it's a spine," he says. "A spine, or thorn, from a poisonous plant."

"From a plant?" says Robin. "Wow! That plant must be a hundred times bigger than any plant I've ever seen!"

Batman looks grim. "If you're right, Boy Wonder, then I'm afraid Poison Ivy has created a monster."

CHAPTER 3

FLORA, FRIENDS AND FOES

Several nights later, moonlight gleams on the glass dome of the Gotham City Botanical Garden.

Inside, swaying trees make dancing shadows.

A young woman dressed in green smiles. "Soon you will all be free," she sings to the plants around her.

Batman and Robin swing down from the dark branches above.

"We knew you'd attack this garden sooner or later," says Robin.

"Attack? Don't be silly," Ivy cries. "This is my kingdom. These are my friends."

"You're heading back to prison," says
Batman. "Say goodbye to your friends."

Poison Ivy tosses her bright red hair and
laughs. "I'm going nowhere," she says. "Say
hello to my newest friend."

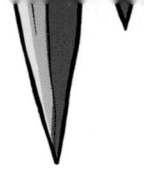

CHAPTER 4

PRISON PLANT

The trees rock back and forth. A large, swaying shadow steps into the moonlight.

"You were right, Robin," says Batman.

The swaying shape is a giant Venus flytrap.

Three giant blossoms snap their deadly jaws. Each blossom has spiny teeth that close tightly like the bars on a prison cell.

A snake-like root shoots forward. It grabs Robin around the waist and lifts him into the air.

With a powerful flick it tosses the Boy Wonder into one of the blossoms. The jaws close around him.

Robin is trapped behind rows of spines as strong as metal bars.

Batman pulls Batarangs from his belt and flings them at the swaying creature.

ZING! ZING!

The Batarangs bounce off the thick, rubbery blossoms.

More roots reach out and wrap tightly around the Caped Crusader.

He is tied and lifted into the air.

HA! HA! HA! HA!

Poison Ivy's laughter echoes through the garden's dome. She stands tall before her foes. Her smile is wide, and her eyes are bright.

"People can be so mean," Ivy says. "But never mind. They can be so tasty too.

"And tonight my flowery friend gets a two-course meal."

The jaws of Robin's prison slowly shut around him. Batman is lifted high above another yawning, hungry blossom.

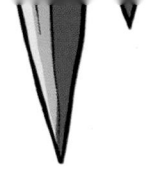

CHAPTER 5

SWEET SMELL OF SUCCESS

"Remember," Ivy says to the Venus flytrap. "Come straight home after dinner!"

The villain picks up a cluster of plants and heads towards an exit door. "You're free, my children," she says to them. "Free!"

Robin pulls a small pellet from his belt.
He quickly throws it through the closing spines
that trap him.

POOF!

The pellet explodes with a small puff of smoke.

"HA!" cries Poison Ivy. "You missed!"

"*Mist* is right," Robin whispers to himself.

Suddenly the flytrap's roots reach out and grab Poison Ivy.

"Put me down!" Ivy commands.

"This monster can't see or hear," says Robin. "So I reckon it must smell its prey."

"That mist smells like a fireproof chemical in our uniforms," explains Batman. "Now you smell like our capes!"

"Save me, Batman!" Ivy screams. "My flytrap can't tell the difference between me and you!"

"If you want your freedom, order it to release all of us," Batman says.

Poison Ivy pouts. Hanging upside down, she knows it's useless to argue.

Ivy closes her eyes and quietly sings a lullaby. Her mind control works.

The Venus flytrap shivers and then obeys. Batman, Robin and Ivy drop to the ground.

Poison Ivy leaps up to dash away, but the Caped Crusader throws a Batarang. It catches the crook with its rope.

"Don't you ever learn, Ivy?" asks Batman.

"That crime doesn't pay?" she says sourly.

"No," says Robin, looking at the jaws of the
Venus flytrap. "That you always bite off more
than you can chew!"

"We got to the *root* of the problem, Robin. So what do we do with this flytrap?"

"We can't just *leaf* it here, Batman."

"Good point. Help me put it in the back of the Batmobile."

"All set, Batman. Now put the *petal* to the metal!"

GLOSSARY

blossom flower on a plant or tree

botanical having to do with plants

device piece of equipment that does a particular job

fireproof does not burn

lullaby gentle song sung to send a baby to sleep

mysterious hard to explain or understand

pellet small, hard ball of something

poisonous able to harm or kill with poison or venom

prey animal hunted by another animal for food

spine hard, sharp, pointed growth such as a thorn or cactus needle

DISCUSS

1. Batman and Robin arrive at Arkham Asylum in their Batmobile. How do you think the Dynamic Duo learned so quickly about Ivy's escape?

2. Why does Poison Ivy want to free the plants from the city's garden? Do you think she is right or wrong?

3. Does the giant Venus flytrap remind you of any other monsters from other stories? Which ones, and how are they the same?

WRITE

1. In the story, we never see the Venus flytrap free Ivy from her prison cell. Write a paragraph explaining how it happened.

2. Batman and Robin use several weapons and tools from their Utility Belts to battle Poison Ivy. If you had a special belt like that, what sort of items would you want in yours? Make a list and describe each one.

3. Poison Ivy, Batman and Robin all wear special uniforms. Imagine you are a super hero or villain. Describe what your uniform looks like and how it helps you in your adventures.

AUTHOR

Michael Dahl is the prolific author of more than 200 other books for children and young adults. He has won the AEP Distinguished Achievement Award three times for his non-fiction, a Teachers' Choice Award from *Learning* magazine and a Seal of Excellence from the Creative Child Awards. He is also the author of the Hocus Pocus Hotel mystery series and the Dragonblood books. Dahl currently lives in Minneapolis, Minnesota, USA.

ILLUSTRATOR

Luciano Vecchio was born in 1982 and is based in Buenos Aires, Argentina. A freelance artist for many projects at Marvel and DC Comics, his work has been seen in print and online around the world. He has illustrated many DC Super Heroes books for Raintree, and some of his recent comic work includes *Beware the Batman*, *Green Lantern: The Animated Series*, *Young Justice*, *Ultimate Spider-Man* and his creator owned web-comic, *Sereno*.